HORRIBLE HARRY
AND
THE PURPLE PEOPLE

HORRIBLE HARRY
AND
THE PURPLE PEOPLE

BY SUZY KLINE
Pictures by Frank Remkiewicz

SCHOLASTIC INC.
New York Toronto London Auckland Sydney

ISBN 0-590-68269-5

Text copyright © 1997 by Suzy Kline.
Illustrations copyright © 1997 by Frank Remkiewicz.
All rights reserved.
Published by Scholastic Inc., 555 Broadway, New York, NY 10012, by arrangement with Viking Penguin, a division of Penguin Books USA Inc.
SCHOLASTIC and associated logos are trademarks and/or registered trademarks of Scholastic Inc.

36 35 34 33   5 6 7 8 9/0

Printed in the U.S.A.   40

First Scholastic printing, October 1998

Set in New Century Schoolbook

Dedicated with love to my students:

Rodney Archer

Arielle Celadon

Marissa De Angelo

Joshua Levesque

Michael Lucas

Sean McDonnell

Eric Mosakowski

Christopher Mosher

Ronnie Noujaim

Christopher Pashley

Katie Poole

Nicole Primerano

Michael Rice

Jeffrey Seiser

Ryan Smith

Raymond Squires

Jacqueline Tribou

Rannan Tyrrell

Melissa Wallace

Mark Woznicki

and my daughter Emily
who shared a very special year

Contents

The Purple People

I'll never forget my last week in second grade.

It was strange.

It was wild.

It all started when Harry showed me his brand-new ruler.

"Hey, Doug," he said, "have you ever seen anything like this?"

I took his ruler and rubbed my hand over it. "Tough wood. It's a lot better than the plastic ones we use at school. I like that row of purple monsters painted at the top."

"They are *not* pictures of monsters. They are pictures of the *Purple People*."

Song Lee, Mary, and Ida overheard us and came over.

"Who are the Purple People?" Mary asked.

"I can't believe you don't know!" Harry replied. "They're brave and strong. And smart."

"And purple," Mary joked. "Pleeeeeease!"

We followed Harry to his desk.

"So," Mary asked, "just . . . where *are* the Purple People?"

Harry motioned with his ruler. "Follow me."

We got in a line and followed Harry around the room—past the science corner, past the teacher's desk, and over to the open window.

Harry closed his eyes and wiggled his fingers. "They're here!"

"Where?" Mary asked.

Harry opened his eyes. "Up there, over here, under there, and in here."

"You're not making any sense, Harry!" Mary snapped.

"I can't help it if I'm the *only one*

who can see the Purple People."

"How many are there?" Sidney asked looking around.

Harry counted them with his ruler.

"There are . . . ten Purple People in Room 2B."

"Ten?" Mary groaned.

"Make that nine," Harry said.

Mary rolled her eyes.

Ida and Song Lee giggled.

"I'm not laughing," Dexter said. "I know about the Purple People."

"You do?" Sidney said. Then he hid behind me.

"Yeah. Someone wrote a rock-and-roll song about them in the fifties. My dad has the record. It goes something like this." Dexter cleared his throat.

"I'm a one-eyed, one-horn, flying purple people-eater—"

"I know that song," Mary interrupted. "It's on one of my tapes. I bet Harry got this whole crazy idea from that song."

Harry shook his head. "Never heard it. I do know the Purple People wouldn't like it though. They'd never buy it."

When the bell rang, we all went to our seats.

Everyone knew Harry had a *huge* imagination but this time he had gone too far. No one believed Harry about his Purple People at first. Not even me. And I'm his best friend.

Miss Mackle picked up her book and continued reading to us about Alice in Wonderland. Alice had just eaten a mushroom, and now her neck had grown so tall it shot out of a tree. All the birds thought she was a snake.

Harry leaned over his desk. I could tell he loved this part.

It didn't make any sense to me. How can you like something you don't understand?

Suddenly a bee flew in the window.

"Look!" Sidney shouted. *"A big bee!"*

Everyone turned around.

Miss Mackle put her book down. "Boys and girls, remain calm. This happens in June." Then she opened her desk drawer and reached for a can of insect spray.

Harry got out his purple ruler and his lunch box. He had his back turned so I couldn't see exactly what he was doing. But he was rubbing something on the ruler.

"Now it's time for the *Purple People* to save our room from doom." He held his ruler up high like it was some kind of a torch.

Bzzzzzzzzzzzz. The bee zoomed around the room. We watched it fly overhead, back and forth. Then . . . suddenly, it landed on Miss Mackle's hair!

Sidney shouted, *"It's going to sting the teacher's head!"*

The class screamed.

Miss Mackle raised her hand. "Shhhhhhhhh."

Harry moved next to the teacher with his ruler. We heard his soft chanting:

> *"Pur-ple Peo-ple*
> *Pur-ple Peo-ple*
> *Save the tea-cher*
> *From the bee!"*

Suddenly, the bee flew off the teacher's head and landed on the purple ruler!

Bzzzzzzzzzz!

Everyone turned pin quiet.

Harry slowly carried the purple ruler over to the open window. The bee clung to it like magic.

Harry dipped the ruler outside the window.

Then he hummed another chant:

> *"Pur-ple Peo-ple*
> *Pur-ple Peo-ple*
> *Shoo the big bee*
> *A-WAY!"*

Five seconds later, the bee let go of the purple ruler and flew away.

The class ooohed and ahhhed as Miss Mackle closed the window.

"Neato!" Sidney said.

The teacher returned to her chair. "Thanks to Harry and his handy ruler, I won't need to use this bug spray. I do need to get a screen for our window."

Mary folded her arms. "Harry and his Purple People! That's *hogwash!*"

"Hogwash?" Miss Mackle replied. "That reminds me of *hooey, balderdash, humbug, poppycock,* and *hokum.* Sometimes we need a little nonsense in our lives. Look at Lewis Carroll who wrote *Alice in Wonderland.* He was a math teacher and he wrote wonderful stories about nonsense."

"Yeah!" Harry replied. Then he fell out of his seat on purpose.

Miss Mackle peered over her reading glasses. "We need a *little* nonsense, Harry," she added.

Harry sat up. He got the teacher's message. "Aren't you going to finish the chapter?" he asked.

"As soon as I find my place."

When she finally did, the only one not listening to the story was Mary.

She kept staring at Harry's desk.

And his ruler that stuck out of it.

"Purple People," Mary grumbled. "Wait till I show Harry how dumb you are!"

The Missing Lunch Card

Thirty minutes later, Miss Mackle started reading the part about the Mad Tea Party. "What a big table with all those place settings and empty seats! Why do you think the March Hare and the Mad Hatter kept changing seats?"

Mary was the only one who raised

her hand. "Because they like changing seats."

"But why?" the teacher asked.

Harry blurted out, "Because they don't have time to do the dishes. They're drinking tea all the time. When they change seats they get clean cups."

Miss Mackle beamed. "You got it, Harry!"

Mary scowled. Then she whispered, "Of course Harry would understand nonsense. If it made sense, he wouldn't understand it."

"Tomorrow," Miss Mackle announced, "we will have a tea party."

"Yeah!" the class cheered.

"I don't like tea," Sidney grumbled.

"I'll make it iced tea," Miss Mackle added. "It is almost summer."

"Can we have real teacups?" Mary asked.

"I'm afraid not," Miss Mackle replied. "But you can write DRINK ME on the paper cups I bring in."

Mary made a face.

"Let's get ready for lunch now," the teacher said.

Those of us who were going to have hot lunch got out our yellow plastic cards with our names on them.

"Hey," Sidney said. "Someone stole my lunch card."

Miss Mackle came over to Sidney's

desk. "You must have dropped it somewhere. Did you take it to another part of the room?"

"Nope. All I did was feed the fish in the science corner."

The teacher went back and looked at the black mollies and the algae eater. "Not here," she said.

Mary cupped her hand over her mouth and whispered, "Maybe the *Purple People* took Sidney's lunch card."

Ida and Song Lee giggled.

Harry turned and glared at Mary. "I heard that. So did . . . the *Purple People!*"

"Oooooooooooh," Mary oohed. "I'm real scared."

"The *Purple People* don't steal things. They find things!" Harry growled.

"I'd like to see them find Sidney's lunch card," Mary snapped.

"They're smart. They can find it."

Slowly, Harry pulled out his purple ruler. He stood up and hummed another chant:

> *"Pur-ple Peo-ple*
> *Pur-ple Peo-ple*
> *Help me find Sid's*
> *Lunch card, pleeeease."*

Harry walked around the room holding the purple ruler. He stopped when he got to the science corner.

"It's not in the tank," Miss Mackle said. "I checked."

Harry got down on his knees and swooped his ruler under the science bookcase. There was about an inch opening between the floor and the bottom shelf.

"The Purple People aren't afraid of dark places," he said.

Then he swooped the ruler again, and something came out from under the bookcase.

Three dust balls and . . .

A yellow plastic lunch card!

Sidney jumped out of his seat.

"There it is!"

Harry picked it off the floor, blew off the dust, and handed it to Sidney.

"Thanks, Harry!" Sidney said.

"Don't thank me," Harry whispered back. "Thank . . . the *Purple People*."

Mary groaned.

"Line up for lunch, boys and girls," Miss Mackle said.

As we lined up, Mary made a point of standing behind Harry. "If those Purple People *really exist,* I dare you to show me one!"

Harry raised his bushy eyebrows. "You want to *meet* one of the Purple People?"

"Yes."

"Okay, Mary. You'll meet one tomorrow."

"When? Where?" Mary demanded.

"At . . ." Harry smiled like the Cheshire Cat . . . "our tea party tomorrow."

"Promise?" Mary said.

"Promise," Harry replied. "Cross my heart, hope to die, stick a needle in my eye."

Mary laughed. "I can't wait!"

Invasion of
the Purple People

At lunch, Mary was whispering stuff
to Ida, Sidney, and Dexter. I knew it
was about Harry. She kept looking at
him when she was whispering.

Harry kept his cool. "She's making
fun of . . . the *Purple People*," he whispered to me.

"Probably," I said.

"She shouldn't do it."

I nodded.

When Mary started to whisper in Song Lee's ear, Song Lee pulled back. "We shouldn't make fun of people," she said.

"But they're not *real* people," Mary said. "They're stupid Purple People."

"They are real to Harry," Song Lee said. "They helped Room 2B. Remember the bee on the teacher's head and Sidney's lunch card?"

"Harry planned all that," Mary replied. "It's just a bunch of hooey, hogwash, balderdash, humbug, poppycock, and hokum."

"What do those words mean?" Song Lee asked.

"Nonsense!" Mary said.

Song Lee patted Mary on the shoulder. "I think you and Harry should be friends. We have only two days of second grade left."

Mary adjusted her glasses. "I *hope* I only have two days more with Harry. He'd better not be in my third grade class!"

Song Lee giggled. "I hope Harry is in my third grade class. He makes me laugh. He has big imagination."

"Big?" Mary replied. "You mean *humongous!*"

At recess, Mary asked to go to the library. "I need to work on a special project," she told us.

I wondered about that special project.

Harry lowered his eyebrows when he saw what Mary took with her.

Purple construction paper, purple clay, and purple yarn.

Thirty minutes later when recess was over, we all went to the water fountain for drinks. Harry and I had forgotten about Mary. We were talking about the kickball game.

"We won," Dexter said.

"*We* won!" Harry replied.

"*We did!*" Dexter said.

"*We did!*" Harry replied.

Song Lee stood behind Harry in line. "We didn't have umpire. It was just practice game. The score doesn't count. Please don't fight."

Miss Mackle smiled at Song Lee. "The world needs more peacemakers like you."

Suddenly, Dexter called out, "I'm bleeding!"

I looked at Dexter. There was blood dripping from his face to the floor.

"Pinch your nose, Dexter," the

teacher said. Then she rushed us all
upstairs. "Go in and sit down, class. I'll
be with you in a minute. I need to take
Dexter to the nurse's room across the

hall. Please stay in your seats."

When we walked into the classroom, we saw it!

The Invasion of the Purple People!

No one sat down.

Six big purple globs of construction paper with purple yarn hair and purple clay eyeballs were stationed in different parts of the room. Each one had a name.

The one in the science corner was HUMBUG. The one next to the window was HOGWASH. The one by the bookcase was HOOEY. POPPYCOCK and BALDERDASH were taped to the blackboard. HOKUM was taped on the back of Harry's seat.

I looked at Harry.

His face turned white, pink, and then bright red!

What was he going to do next?

Turn purple?

Purple Monsters, Purple People, and a Floating Head

Harry held up a fist. "*Those* are purple *monsters*. They are not the real Purple People!"

Mary put her hands on her hips. "What do they look like, then?"

"People," Harry said. "They just happen to be purple."

"And *invisible*," Mary grumbled.

"So? They prefer being invisible, but tomorrow . . . I've invited one to *come out* . . . at the tea party!" Harry said through his gritted teeth.

"I can't wait," Mary said.

When the teacher showed up at the door, everyone plopped down in their chair.

"Well, I see my old friends Humbug, Hogwash, Hooey, Hokum, Balderdash, and Poppycock are joining our class."

"Do you want me to take them down?" Mary asked politely.

"No, I think they're cute. They liven up our last week of school."

Harry made a fist on his desk.

"Dexter is fine," the teacher added. "He just had a bad nose bleed. Now, let's see how Alice is doing in her croquet game."

As Miss Mackle picked up her book and continued reading, Harry's fist unfolded. He leaned forward again on his desk and listened to the story.

He laughed when Alice played croquet with a flamingo for a mallet and a
live hedgehog for a ball!

When Miss Mackle read the part about the Cheshire Cat and the Queen of Hearts saying, "Off with his head," she waited a moment for Harry.

He had to repeat the words. "Off with his head! Off with his head!"

Miss Mackle didn't get mad. She didn't mind a little nonsense.

Mary raised her hand. "That's dumb. You can't chop off someone's head if it doesn't have a body. The Cheshire Cat was just a floating head."

"Off with *her* head!" Harry said pointing to Mary.

"Very funny," Mary grumbled. "We'll see who's laughing tomorrow at the tea party, Harry, when you introduce me to one of those so-called Purple People."

"It'll be my pleasure," Harry said, flashing his white teeth.

Mary Meets One of the Purple People

The next morning, Sidney arrived wearing a black hat with a joker card on it. "I'm the Mad Hatter," he said, laughing.

"Cool," I said. "Look's like Ida is Alice. She's wearing a white apron and white socks, and she's got a white stuffed rabbit.

"What did you bring, Harry?" I asked.

"Grape juice and a hand mirror. What did you bring, Doug?"

I opened up a tin box. "Mom and I made cookies. See?"

"What fun!" Ida said. "Each one says, EAT ME!"

Song Lee set a vase on the table. "Wonderland has so many gardens. I picked flowers for our table."

We looked at the snapdragons, pinks, marigolds, and daisies.

"Look!" Ida said. "There's a caterpillar on one of the flowers."

Mary looked closely. "It's not real."

"It's the Caterpillar from *Alice in*

Wonderland," Song Lee said. "See the little clay hookah I made for his pipe?"

"Smoking is bad for you," Mary complained. "We shouldn't have a pipe at our tea."

Then Mary took the little clay pipe, squished it, and put it in her dress pocket.

"Ohhhhh!" Ida gasped. "That's mean!"

Song Lee looked down at her shoes. "It . . . it was in the story."

Harry glared at Mary. "Off with her head!" he said.

"Off with her head!" I repeated.

Song Lee covered her mouth when she started to giggle, but we heard her.

After lunch, we arranged the desks
and chairs in a circle. We made place
mats and passed out paper plates and
paper cups with handles. Miss Mackle

passed out napkins that had a playing
card on each one. I got a jack.

Mary opened her book bag and took
out her own china teacup. It was about

the size of a walnut. "It's from my own tea set," she bragged.

Song Lee picked up her paper cup. "I can pretend this is real china too." Then she began coloring cherry blossoms on it.

Mary looked at Harry's place. "Hey," she complained, "how come he gets the queen card on his napkin?"

"Because I get to say, *'Off with her head!'*"

Mary rolled her eyes, then stopped when she noticed something else. "How come you get *two* paper cups?"

"One's for me," Harry replied. "The other is . . . for one of the *Purple People*. You're meeting her at the tea party. I saved a seat for her."

"It's a *her?*" Mary asked.

"Or a she," Harry replied. "Don't you know there are girl Purple People and boy Purple People?"

Mary shook her head. Then she tried to sit down next to Song Lee.

"I'm sorry," Song Lee said. "I'm sitting next to Ida and Harry at the tea party."

Mary's eyes bulged. "And not me?"

Song Lee nodded.

"Why not?" Mary asked.

Song Lee shrugged.

"I'll tell you why," I said. "The past week, you've been zero fun. You've hurt people's feelings. You've made fun of people, even *Purple People!*"

Mary bit her lip.

"Oh, be quiet, Doug. You don't know anything."

Reluctantly, Mary sat down on the other side of Harry.

Slowly, she got that squished piece of clay out of her dress pocket, shaped it into a small hookah again, and placed it back in the bouquet of flowers.

Then it happened.

Harry got ready to introduce Mary to one of the Purple People.

"Okeydokey, Mary!" he sang. And he pulled out a hand mirror. "Hold this, Doug."

I raised my eyebrows.

When Harry picked up his thermos

and poured some grape juice, I could see how *purple* it was.

I knew what Harry was about to do! Oh no!

Harry was going to be in big trouble.

Not just with the teacher, but with Song Lee, too! This was more than a *little* nonsense.

I knew I had to think fast!

Harry turned to Mary. He held the paper cup of grape juice in his hand. I stood next to Mary and held the mirror.

"Mary," Harry said. "you are about to meet one of the Purple People."

Mary looked up at Harry.

This was going to be a direct hit.

Song Lee was watching when Harry raised his cup and started to tip it over Mary's hair and face.

Quickly, I ducked in front of Mary.

Kersplooooooooosh!

I could taste the grape juice as it dripped down my hair and into my face. "Mary," I said, "meet one of the Purple People."

Harry's eyes bulged. "But . . ."

Mary and Song Lee giggled.

Then Mary held out her hand, and I shook it. "I thought I was meeting a girl Purple People?" she said.

I licked some grape juice off my mouth. "Slight change of plans."

"Nice to meet you," Mary said.

Song Lee shook my hand, too.

Harry got a paper towel and started wiping my purple face and hair. "I'm sorry, man. It was supposed to be for—"

"Me?" Mary said.

Harry shrugged.

"Thanks, Doug," Mary said. "I guess I have been a real wet blanket."

"Not as wet as I am now," I joked.

Just as everyone laughed, Miss Mackle came rushing over. "Someone spill something?"

No one tattled.

Not even Mary.

"It was just an accident," I said.

"Okay then, everyone ready?" Miss Mackle said. "Let's hold up our teacups and make our Wonderland toast.

"To . . . Alice!" Miss Mackle said.

"To . . . the Cheshire Cat," Sidney added.

"To . . . the Caterpillar," Song Lee said.

"To . . . the White Rabbit," I said.

"To . . . the Purple People," Harry said.

"And to . . . *a little* balderdash," Mary said.

And then we all clicked our teacups.